Bizarre Murders

Gilda and Melvin Berger

Bizarre Murders

Julian Messner New York

Published by Julian Messner, a Simon & Schuster
Division of Gulf & Western Corporation.
Simon & Schuster Building,
1230 Avenue of the Americas,
New York, New York 10020.

JULIAN MESSNER and colophon are trademarks of
Simon & Schuster

Manufactured in the United States of America

Design by Irving Perkins Associates

Library of Congress Cataloging in Publication Data

Berger, Gilda.
  Bizarre murders.

  Bibliography: p.
  Includes index.
  Summary: Accounts of unusual murders, both historical
and contemporary. Includes the crimes of Jack the
Ripper, Leopold and Loeb, and Charles Manson.
  1. Murder—Great Britain—History—Juvenile
literature. 2. Murder—United States—History—
Juvenile literature. 3. Murder—Great Britain—Case
studies—Juvenile literature. 4. Murder—United
States—Case studies—Juvenile literature. [1. Murder—
Case studies] I. Berger, Melvin. II. Title.
HV6535.G4B47 1983   364.1′523′0942   82-42880
ISBN 0-671-45583-4

Contents

1 Murder – Bizarre Style   9

2 Burke and Hare: Bodies for Sale   12

3 Jack the Ripper   17

4 Lizzie Borden   24

5 Thomas Bram: Murder on the High Seas   30

6 Dr. Crippen   36

7 Leopold and Loeb: The Crime of the
   Century   41

8 The Murder Gang: Five Frustrated Killers   50

9 Nannie Doss: A Romantic at Heart   53

10 Albert DeSalvo: The Boston Strangler   57

11 Richard Speck: "Born to Raise Hell"   62

12 Charles Manson: Helter-Skelter   66

13 Peter Sutcliffe: The Yorkshire Ripper   73

14 David Berkowitz: Son of Sam   81

   Bibliography   89

   Index   91

Bizarre Murders

Chapter 1

Murder – Bizarre Style

BODY FOUND MISSING HEAD AND ARMS
CRAZED KILLER SLAYS 16
POLICE UNCOVER MURDER FACTORY
THRILL KILLER AT LARGE
TORTURE VICTIM SLAIN IN PARK
MILD-MANNERED MURDERER STRIKES AGAIN

EACH OF THESE newspaper headlines describes a bizarre murder—one that is especially strange, odd, or unusual. While there is no such thing as a usual or ordinary murder, a certain number stand out as being more grotesque, brutal, or weird than most others.

Take the story of Joe Ball and his alligators. Ball was the owner of a restaurant outside San Antonio, Texas. The eatery was famous for its good southern food and lavish decor. Also well known were its attractive waitresses in their skimpy uniforms and the alligator pool behind the dining room. From time to time, though, customers complained that their favorite waitresses were no longer working there. Joe usually said it was because they had quit to take other jobs.

In 1938 the real reason some waitresses had vanished came to light. A witness testified that he saw Joe choke a young woman to death in the kitchen, grab a butcher's cleaver, hack the body into small pieces—and feed the bits to the alligators! Joe died at his own hands, too. When the Texas Rangers arrived to arrest him, Joe snatched a gun from a drawer and killed himself on the spot.

Then there is the extraordinary case of eighteen-year-old Penny Bjorkland who seemed blessed with good looks and great fortune. For some reason, on February 1, 1959, Penny awoke saying to herself, "This is the day I will kill someone."

Penny took a target-practice pistol from its rack and left her house. When a passing motorist offered her a ride, she slid into the front seat, yanked out the gun, and pumped six bullets into the driver's head and body. After jumping out, and dashing around to the other side of the car, she unloaded six more bullets into his dead form. Dragging the corpse from the car, Penny fired six additional slugs into the bleeding remains. When asked in a prison interview what kind of person she was, Penny said, "I consider myself a normal, average girl."

College student and ex-marine Charles Whitman went berserk on July 31, 1966. He began by shooting his mother and stabbing his wife. Next he locked himself on the roof of a tower at the University of Texas with a number of pistols and rifles and a supply of ammunition. He shot at everyone who came within range, killing a total of sixteen and wounding thirty. His murder spree did not end until the police stormed the tower and cut him down with a barrage of bullets.

Herman Drenth was a salesman of used furniture in Clarksburg, West Virginia; his sideline was murder. Starting in 1921 Drenth sought out wealthy widows from all over the country. After courting and marrying each one, he brought her to his "scientific laboratory" in the woods near Clarksburg. Once inside, he tied his bride's hands and feet, and left. Then he released a poison gas into the room and watched the woman expire. When she was dead, the scoundrel stole all of her money and valuables and buried the body in the surrounding woods. Over a period of ten years Drenth killed more than fifty wives in this systematic—and yes, bizarre—way.

The cases of murder you will read in this book are all bizarre. They may shock, horrify, or frighten you. But what may disturb you most of all is the fact that they are all absolutely true!

Chapter 2

Burke and Hare: Bodies for Sale

Log's BOARDING HOUSE, in the early 1800s, was located in the dreary, squalid slums of Edinburgh, Scotland. For three pence a night, lodgers received shelter in one of three cramped, dingy, foul-smelling rooms in the cellar of a dilapidated house. The eight beds, covered with rotting, discolored straw mattresses, were oft-times shared by two or even more unlucky souls.

In the chilly late autumn of 1827, one regular guest at Log's, an old army veteran called Donald, with no known family ties, took seriously ill. Day after day, his condition worsened. On November 29 he died.

Maggie Log, owner of the rooming establishment, and her boyfriend, William Hare, didn't know what to do. Donald owed four pounds in back rent. And to make matters worse, there was no one to pay the cost of a coffin and burial.

Another boarder, William Burke, had an idea. Instructors of surgery at the University of Edinburgh medical school, he told Hare, needed bodies for teaching purposes. They were paying as much as ten pounds for each corpse they got in good condition. Since Donald owed so much money and his body wouldn't be missed by anyone, why not sell it to one of the professors of medicine?

Hare seized the notion and lost no time in acting on it. With Burke, he found a large, empty tea chest, stuffed the corpse inside, and carried it off to Surgeon's Square, the distinguished center of the medical profession in Edinburgh. A few enquiries brought them to No. 10 Surgeon's Square, the residence of Dr. Robert Knox.

Dr. Knox was a very popular and highly successful private teacher of anatomy and surgery. Soon after Burke and Hare brought their tea-box coffin into his gloomy morgue, the doctor examined it. Delighted to receive the specimen, he paid the two men the munificent sum of seven pounds ten shillings. What's more, he told them he'd be interested in getting as many more bodies as they could provide—with no questions asked.

For a short while the men were sorely tempted to become body snatchers—individuals who robbed undertakers and dug up fresh graves to meet doctors' need for bodies to use for dissection. But then reason prevailed and they decided against joining those ranks. Regretfully they resumed their beggarly occupations. Burke went back to finding old shoes, repairing and selling them. Hare continued peddling herrings from a pushcart.

Presently, a different lodger at Log's, Joseph by name, became sick. The poor man ran a very high fever, and as his malady dragged on, word of it spread. Many regular lodgers took accommodations elsewhere. Hare bewailed his poor fortune. Not only wasn't Joseph paying his three pence a night but he was driving away the other clients. ·

Before things got any worse, Burke and Hare

hatched a fearful plan. They would put an end to Joseph's suffering and turn it to a profit at the same time. The short, mean Burke threw himself on top of the ailing man. At the same time, the big, powerful Hare pressed a grubby pillow over the sufferer's face. For about ten minutes Joseph thrashed about wildly. Then suddenly he stopped breathing and grew very still.

The partners in crime hunched over his body and squeezed it into the tea chest. Under the cover of darkness, they delivered it to Dr. Knox's address. This time the doctor rewarded them with a ten pound note.

It wasn't long before the entire amount was spent on gin and whiskey. The lure of fast, easy money to end their impecunious state became irresistible. The shoe repairer and herring peddler decided to go into business. Together they would meet the need for bodies more quickly than nature had provided. They would turn to murder.

By night, Burke and Hare prowled the dark, narrow alleys of Edinburgh's slum seeking likely victims. Drunks and derelicts were enticed to the rooming house basement with the promise of free drinks. The cohorts kept the visitors' glasses full, until they fell into a stupor. Then, while Burke pinned them to the floor or bed, Hare clamped his hamlike hand over the hapless ones' mouth and nose until death came.

In the course of nine months, Dr. Knox received about sixteen bodies from the greedy twosome. Among the duped were a nameless salesman from England; a seller of salt named Abigail Simpson; an old woman, Mary Hadane; Mary's daughter Peggy; a prostitute, Mary Paterson; and several whose identities were never discovered.

Business was booming, and the prosperous Burke

and Hare now employed a porter to take the deliveries to Surgeon's Square. And, instead of operating only at night, they began to carry on their barbarous work boldly during the daytime hours as well.

On one occasion, Burke was out looking for a "shot" as the victims were called. He came upon an elderly beggar woman and her deaf grandson. In response to his offers of food and lodging, the lady and child followed him back to the rooming house. Once there, the murderers attacked them and soon arranged the double shipment to Dr. Knox.

Moved more and more by their desire for money, the grasping Burke and Hare became increasingly careless. In October 1828, their victim was "Daft Jamie," a lame, mentally retarded eighteen-year-old, who was a familiar figure in the community. Neighbors whispered amongst themselves when they saw Burke's nephew wearing the missing Jamie's clothes. And some of Dr. Knox's students suspected foul play when they beheld Jamie on the dissecting table. Still, no one brought any charges against the impudent killers.

Mary Docherty was another "shot" whose demise did not go entirely unnoticed. When Burke arrived at the basement murder factory with Mary in tow, a couple named Gray, who were there, were asked to leave. As soon as the Grays were gone, the two men noisily and roughly knocked Mary out with a blow to the head and then throttled her in the usual way.

The Grays returned late the next afternoon, before the killers had time to arrange for shipment of the body to Dr. Knox. When the couple lay down on the bed, in the basement room they discovered Mary's body stuffed into the straw mattress. In a panic, they rushed out to inform the police.

While they were gone, Burke and Hare returned to cram Mary's body into the tea chest for conveyance by the porter. Just as the two were ready to leave for a night on the town, the Grays returned with the police. Mary's body was gone, but a search of the room turned up fresh blood stains on the bedding. The men were arrested.

In due course, Hare and Burke were brought to trial. Before the date of the hearing, Hare offered to confess all in return for immunity from prosecution. His request was granted.

The hearing ran twenty-four hours without stop. Hare detailed for the court the entire story of the bodies-for-sale scheme, from the first delivery of Donald's corpse to the last murder of Mary Docherty.

It took less than an hour for the jury to return a verdict of guilty. Burke was hanged at dawn on January 28, 1829 before a crowd estimated at 25,000. All the others involved in the mercenary plot—Hare and Dr. Knox included—got off scot free.

Chapter 3

Jack the Ripper

ON THE FOGGY night of August 31, 1888, an English constable was walking his beat in the twisting, dark courts and alleys of London's East End. He stumbled over the dead form of a woman. She was lying on her back, and her dress was pulled up above her knees. Her throat was cut from ear to ear. Further examination showed several severe slashes in her abdomen. There was no sign of a struggle.

The body was identified as that of Mary Ann Nichols, thirty-eight years old, separated from her husband for nine years and known in the East End for heavy drinking and immoral behavior. The police had not the slightest clue to the murderer's identity.

Eight days later the murderer struck again in the same dismal, forbidding district of London. Another woman was found in the back yard of a dilapidated old house. Her throat was jaggedly cut and her stomach ripped completely open. The intestines had been removed and wrapped around the woman's neck.

The victim was found to be Annie Chapman. She was a prostitute who frequented the common lodging houses in the area, often drunk and dressed in tattered, dirty clothes. It seemed clear that the same person had committed both murders.

17

SKETCHES AT THE INQUEST

A police constable discovering the body of Mary Ann Nichols, the first victim of Jack the Ripper.

The scene of the next crime was a gloomy court enshrouded in darkness; the time, the early morning hours of September 30. Found dead was Elizabeth Stride, a middle-aged prostitute. Apparently lured into that court, the victim had been deeply gashed. The owner of a nearby fruit stand said he had sold Liz Stride three pennies' worth of grapes not ten minutes before her body was found. Her companion at that time, he said, was stocky, wore a battered slouch hat and a greatcoat, and carried a little black doctor's bag.

A short while later on that same night, a second body was discovered in the darkest corner of Mitre Square, about a block from where Stride was found. This victim's name was Catherine Eddowes. Her body had been even more viciously attacked than those of the others. Besides cutting her throat, the killer had slashed her face, carving away parts of her nose and right ear. The abdomen had been ripped open and her kidneys removed.

Confounding the police in the Eddowes case was the fact that fifteen minutes earlier a police constable had passed the very spot where the body was found. He saw nothing unusual. Also, Catherine had been seen with a man wearing a greatcoat and carrying a small black bag. Statements by Scotland Yard suggested that the killer was a man with medical knowledge. Who else could slash and surgically remove the organs from a victim in less than fifteen minutes?

After the double murder of Stride and Eddowes, a group of citizens called the Vigilance Committee formed to combat the terrifying wave of killings. A short while later the president of the committee received half a kidney, a bloody fingerprint, and a note signed, "Jack the Ripper." Within hours a newspaper got a similar letter with the same signature. Both ended with the dare, "Catch me when you can."

Like a fire raging in a tinderbox, the name Jack the Ripper spread through London. Fear and panic followed close behind. The dreary, dim, gaslit alleys and cobblestone streets of the East End were virtually deserted. Prostitutes in particular did not venture out. They huddled together inside their crumbling rooming houses. The police arrested, questioned, and released for lack of evidence over 150 men.

For over a month there were no more slayings. Then the killer struck again. This time it was the horrendous death and mutilation of Mary Jane Kelly on November 9. The victim, another prostitute, was a girl in her teen years. The crime was committed indoors, in the room where she had been living for some months. Mary Kelly's body was so horribly slashed and torn that witnesses reported that she could barely be made out to be human.

With the death of the unfortunate girl, the murderous activities of Jack the Ripper stopped as suddenly and mysteriously as they had begun. Soon afterward, Sir Melville Macnaghten of Scotland Yard announced his belief that Montague John Druitt was Jack the Ripper. Born in August 1857, Druitt was a star cricket player in school. After graduation he first became a lawyer and then a teacher.

Druitt disappeared right after Mary Jane Kelly's death. According to Macnaghten, Druitt's family thought him "sexually insane" and believed he was guilty. On December 4 Druitt's body was found in the Thames River. His pockets were filled with stones, and he was declared a suicide. It was two months since the last killing. The medical report estimated that his body had been in the water about the same length of time.

But there were some problems with Macnaghten's report. For one thing, it would have been almost impossible for Druitt to have killed the women and still have been present at the cricket matches that he played on the following days. Yet many people accepted Macnaghten's argument. They said the killer should be known as Montague the Ripper.

The matter remained somewhat clouded until mid-1970, when a new and startling theory on the identity of Jack the Ripper came to light. England's TV network, the BBC, and an investigative reporter brought out an explanation that reached all the way up to Buckingham

Palace and the British royal family. There wasn't a single Jack the Ripper, they held. Rather, three men sent out by Queen Victoria, the all-powerful monarch at the time, were responsible for the dastardly murders.

The main source of information was the English artist Joseph Sickert. His father, Walter Sickert, had been a prominent painter during the reign of Queen Victoria.

The story passed down by the older Sickert was this:

In 1884 he was asked by Princess Alexandra, daughter-in-law of the queen, to teach art to her rather slow and untalented son, the Duke of Clarence, who was known as Eddy. Lessons were to be conducted in private, with special care that Queen Victoria not hear of it.

The instruction started, and Eddy came whenever he could safely escape from the palace. During the summer of 1884 Sickert introduced Eddy to Annie Elizabeth Crook, a young woman who worked in a nearby tobacco shop and sometimes modeled for him. Annie and Eddy immediately fell in love, and not long afterward Annie became pregnant. The baby, a girl named Alice Margaret Crook, was born the following April.

The entire matter was, of course, kept secret. A friend of Annie's, named Mary Jane Kelly, cared for the infant while the mother continued working. In time, though, the truth leaked out, and the news reached the queen. Victoria wanted the matter hushed up and forgotten. But her prime minister, the Marquess of Salisbury, arranged a "raid" to bring Eddy back to the palace and to place Annie in a lunatic asylum. The marquess feared that if the facts were revealed the socialists and republicans would use the incident to stir up a revolution that might overthrow the monarchy.

The baby stayed with Mary Jane Kelly and thus es-

The scene of the last Ripper murder in the Whitechapel district of London.

caped Salisbury's thugs. But soon there came talk that Kelly had fallen in with a group of East End prostitutes who were hatching a scheme to collect blackmail for Kelly's silence. Salisbury could not tolerate this situation. He devised a plan to silence permanently Kelly and her three friends—Mary Ann Nichols, Annie Chapman, and Elizabeth Stride.

Sir William Gull, Queen Victoria's physician, was given the gruesome task. Helping him was Sir Robert Anderson, a close friend and assistant commissioner of the Metropolitan Police. Also in on the plot was coachman John Netley, who earlier had driven Eddy to his secret art lessons and meetings with Annie.

The operation started on August 31. Mary Ann Nichols was walking the streets when the two well-dressed gentlemen enticed her into their carriage. There they quickly ripped open her throat and tossed her body out when the deed was done. Chapman was killed in the same way.

Since Elizabeth Stride was too drunk to understand their invitation, Netley and Anderson left the carriage, and Netley slit her throat on the street. In their haste they did not perform the mutilation that was part of the other slayings.

The next killing, that of Catherine Eddowes, was done in error. The three assassins thought that she was Kelly, since she sometimes used that name. Because Kelly was believed to be at the heart of the entire affair, the killers reserved the most brutal and sadistic slaying for her.

Later they discovered their mistake. After waiting a while, they set out again to murder the real Mary Jane Kelly. Their task done, the Jack-the-Ripper killings ceased.

Yet the speculations surrounding the brutal murders of the five London prostitutes continued for almost a century. No murders have been the subject of more books, plays, and movies than those of Jack the Ripper. Although no one was caught at the time, some are satisfied that we now know the true killers. Others say the matter will remain veiled in mystery forever.

Chapter 4

Lizzie Borden

ON AUGUST 4, 1892, a particularly brutal double murder occurred in the stately Borden house in Fall River, Massachusetts. At about nine-thirty that morning a killer viciously attacked Abby Borden, the wife of one of the wealthiest men in Fall River, as she was making the bed in an upstairs guest room. With great force and energy the murderer smashed in her face with several blows of a hatchet. The dead woman's battered form was left where it fell on the spare room floor.

Later that same morning, around eleven o'clock, Andrew Jackson Borden returned home from his business to rest and eat lunch. Borden not only controlled several cotton mills and banks but also looked after his large holdings in the street railway and in real estate.

As was his habit, Borden went first to the sitting room and stretched out on the sofa for a short nap before his meal. While he slept, the killer approached, and with even more power and might than had been used on Mrs. Borden, dealt him ten hatchet blows to the face, turning it into a mass of bloody pulp.

Lizzie Borden, the thirty-two-year-old unmarried daughter of Andrew Borden and stepdaughter of Abby Borden, found the two bodies some time that afternoon. Lizzie sent the servant, Bridget Sullivan, to fetch the doctor and to notify the police.

In the investigation that followed, the detectives found out that Lizzie and Bridget were at home that fateful morning. Bridget claimed that she was working in the back of the house and saw and heard nothing. The police questioned her closely and, convinced of her innocence, did not examine her any further.

Lizzie, however, was quizzed at far greater length. With the utmost respect for her high social position in the town, the police proceeded cautiously.

They asked her where she was at the time of her father's death. Lizzie replied that she was in the barn for about ten minutes. Later she said it might have been fifteen or perhaps even twenty minutes. Long enough, in any case, to have missed the killing.

To explain the long time she stayed in the barn, Lizzie recalled munching on pears and looking out the window. Another time she changed her story and said that maybe she didn't look out the window after all.

At one point it came out that Lizzie had been ill the morning of the crimes and had not eaten breakfast. Well then, the question arose, why would she eat pears when she was sick? The answer was matter-of-fact: she just wanted to.

As to the reason why she was in the barn, the woman said she had gone there to find lead to make sinkers so she could go fishing. When it turned out that she hadn't gone fishing in five years, Lizzie told instead how she had gone to the barn to get screening to repair a window.

How did she explain the testimony of three witnesses who saw her buy the deadly poison, prussic acid, on that same morning? Prussic acid, she responded haughtily, has nothing to do with hatchet murders.

Was she concerned about not having seen or heard her stepmother all through that August morning? Lizzie recounted how a boy had brought a note from a sick

Lizzie Borden.

friend of Mrs. Borden (Lizzie called her stepmother that, even after twenty-five years), and she just assumed that Mrs. Borden had gone to visit her. When informed that the police had not been able to locate the boy, the note, or the sick friend, Lizzie merely shrugged.

Lizzie's answers left investigators confused. Was she guilty or innocent? And if neither she nor Bridget killed Mr. and Mrs. Borden, then who did?

Lizzie told of threats from the helpers on her father's farm. She said that she also saw some mysterious men lurking near their house. And she recalled that several times Mrs. Borden had expressed the fear that the entire family was being poisoned.

The police explored Lizzie's relationship with her father. While not the richest Borden in Fall River, he was still worth over a quarter of a million dollars. But as good as he was at making money, he was far better at saving it. He and his family lived more modestly than any of the other Bordens. Lizzie grumbled that she wanted a larger house in the more fashionable Hill district of town. She longed for fancier clothes and a grand carriage in which to go calling on her cousins. Her father, however, preferred to pinch pennies and see his fortune grow, rather than provide such luxuries.

Saturday, August 6, was the day of the funeral. Lizzie attended her parents' burial, primly dressed in black mourning clothes. Meanwhile, their suspicions aroused, the police searched the house. They were seeking blood-stained clothing and the murder weapon, but they found neither. The next day, though, when a friend came to pay a sympathy call, she found Lizzie burning a dress. Lizzie explained that she was getting rid of it because of old paint stains.

Based on all the circumstantial evidence, Lizzie was charged with the double slaying and made to stand trial. The inquiry, which began on June 3, 1893, lasted thir-

The back of the Borden home in Fall River. The building on the right is the barn.

teen days. As the trial went on, Lizzie showed more and more emotion. Several times she cried and even fainted. Often she asked for water and sniffed at her smelling salts. When entering or leaving the courtroom she leaned heavily on railings for support.

The sympathy of the court—the three judges, the jury, even the prosecution lawyer—was aroused by the "poor, defenseless girl," as Lizzie was often called. Even when it was brought out that Lizzie was angered by her father's miserly ways, that she hated her stepmother intensely, and that she greedily looked forward to receiving her inheritance, she was still regarded with pity. The prosecutor's argument that it was next to impossible that an outside killer would want to destroy both Mr. and Mrs. Borden was poorly received. His reasoning that no outsider would be able to kill Mrs. Borden, hide for an hour and half, and then kill Mr. Borden without being discovered was largely ignored.

At the trial's end, the all-male jury was absent from the courtroom for only one hour before they brought back the verdict: not guilty. It later came out that they had unanimously agreed on that decision in the first ballot. They had just waited for an hour so it would seem as though they had deliberated.

Public opinion was much less kind. Most people considered Lizzie Borden guilty of the hatchet murders of her parents. For the remaining thirty-five years of her life, children and some adults, too, taunted her with the now famous verse:

> Lizzie Borden took an ax
> And gave her mother forty whacks;
> When she saw what she had done,
> She gave her father forty-one.

Legally freed of responsibility for the crime, Lizzie and her older sister Emma, who had been away at the time of the killings, divided the large inheritance. Lizzie bought a fine house on the Hill and a carriage befitting one of her wealth and position. Both sisters died in 1927, within one week of each other.

Many books and articles, several plays, an opera, and a ballet have been written expressing various views of the hatchet murders and the outcome of the trial. The popular opinion now seems to be that Lizzie Borden was indeed guilty of murder. She was declared innocent, some say, because she was a woman who cried and fainted in court. The fact that she had neither a husband nor a father to stand by her side also worked in her favor. Her prominent family background helped as well. If Lizzie Borden was indeed guilty, then she is one of the few people ever to commit a bizarre murder and get away with it.

Chapter 5

Thomas Bram: Murder on the High Seas

THE *HERBERT FULLER* set sail from Boston Harbor on Friday, July 3, 1896, bound for the port of Rosario, Argentina, with a heavy cargo of lumber. According to an old belief of seamen, a voyage begun on Friday will encounter trouble—storm, shipwreck, mutiny, or even murder. What happened aboard the *Herbert Fuller* between Boston and Rosario served to strengthen that belief.

It was calm and peaceful for the first ten days of the *Fuller's* voyage. But on the night of July 13 a series of gruesome events shattered the calm.

Lester Monks, a Harvard student, was fast asleep in his cabin. Monks had signed on as the freighter's only passenger in the hope that the sea air would restore his failing health. Sometime in the middle of that night Monks was awakened by a woman's shrill scream. The only woman on board was Laura, the wife of Charles Nash, the captain of the ship.

Monks leaped down from his bunk and seized the pistol he kept under his pillow. As quickly as possible he made his way to the chart house on the main deck where the captain usually slept. There was no light in the chart house, and Monks had trouble moving about. Hearing a gurgling sound, he hastened in the direction of the noise. In his rush he stumbled over a body. It was the captain who was making these strangulated cries. Monks bent over and touched the ship's commander just as the old man died. When Monks pulled back his hand, it was warm and sticky with freshly spilled blood.

Recalling the screams he had heard, Monks hurried to Mrs. Nash's cabin below deck. The woman was lying in a pool of blood in her bunk. She had been hacked to death. Her skull was smashed in, and there were deep gashes all over her body.

Monks had only one thought: find someone with whom to share his frightful discoveries. He located First Mate Thomas Bram and brought him to the scenes of the two tragedies. For a long while, Bram looked on without saying a word, his face clouded with fear.

In a trembling voice Bram told Monks that the two deaths signaled the start of a mutiny, probably led by Second Mate August Blomberg. He recalled Blomberg giving him a drink of whiskey from a metal cup and then tossing the cup over the side. Bram said he suspected that the drink was poisoned because it made him sick. He backed up his charge by pointing out a splash of vomit on the wooden deck.

Both men sat on the top deck awaiting the first rays of dawn. Then Monks, Bram, and the steward, Jonathan Spencer, went to assess the damage. The captain and his wife were sprawled out, brutally and savagely killed by many blows to the face, head, and body. Looking around, they noticed that Blomberg's cabin door was open. The second mate lay on the bunk, his head bashed in and his body covered in blood. Blomberg had suffered the same fate as the other two.

The three men went up on deck, away from the mass slayings. When they came midship, near the mainmast, Bram suddenly squinted and pointed to a spot on the opposite side of the deck.

"There's an ax," he shouted. "That's the ax that did it."

Neither of the other men saw it. But Bram leaped across the deck, tossed aside some planks that lay there, and pulled out an ax still shiny with blood.

"Shall I throw it overboard?" Bram asked.

Spencer started to say no, but it was too late. Bram had already sent it spinning into the churning water below.

Having aroused Spencer's suspicions by this action, Bram proceeded to relate his theory of the mutiny and the doctored drink Bromberg had given him. Now he wanted to show him where he had thrown up.

"We'll put some of that into a bottle and have it examined when we reach port," Spencer said.

Bram agreed and started forward to collect a sample but appeared to trip and step in it. As he wiped it off his shoe, he destroyed still another important clue.

Legally Bram, as first mate, was now in charge of the vessel, but he acted weak and oddly confused. He called the crew together but could do nothing to quiet their fears that a mad-dog killer was still on the boat. Optimistically, Bram told them they should put the murders behind them and act just like a happy family. The men, though, remained suspicious and distrustful of one another.

Bram offered Monks this explanation of what had happened:

Blomberg had tried to rape Mrs. Nash. Captain Nash came to his wife's defense, and Blomberg killed them both. An unknown fourth person, seeing the situation, had killed Blomberg. The second mate somehow made it back to his cabin bunk before dying.

Monks wrote up a full account of the events and characters on the *Herbert Fuller*, including Bram's theory. Every member of the crew read and signed the document.

Tension on the ship continued to grow as they headed back toward port. Ill at ease and nervous from living in constant fear, no one was able to sleep. One night, a crew member named Julius Westerburg was seen throwing a pair of blood-stained trousers overboard. The men in the crew grabbed Westerburg and chained him in his cabin despite his claims that his pants became stained while he was helping to move the bodies.

After the capture of Westerburg, Bram directed Monks to tear up and throw away the murder account signed earlier, since now they had the real killer. Monks refused.

From his cell, Westerburg called Monks and the seamen together before the ship reached port. The sailor told them a startling story.

On the night of the slayings, he related, he saw Bram enter the chart house and hack away at Captain Nash. A few minutes later he heard Mrs. Nash's shriek. From his hiding place he could see Bram come up on deck carrying something that might have been the bloody ax.

Monks and the crew members, swayed by Westerburg's account, now seized Bram and bound him to the mast.

Six days later the *Herbert Fuller* crept into Boston harbor with its sad cargo of three corpses and two prisoners in chains. The grand jury examined Westerburg and ordered him to be set free. They decided to hold Bram for a trial starting on December 14, 1896.

During the cross-examination, Bram was confronted by Westerburg's statement that he had attacked Nash. Bram replied to the accusation in a most damaging way.

"He could not have seen me. Where was he?" he said.

Bram's other very suspicious acts were also brought out at the lengthy trial: his claims of a mutiny that did not exist; the charges he leveled first against Blomberg and then against Westerburg; his discovery of the murder weapon and then his tossing it overboard; his destruction of evidence that he had been drugged; and his efforts to do away with the account Monks had written.

The prosecution brought forth other witnesses who testified that Bram had railed at Captain Nash near the start of the voyage saying that his wife should "be taken care of by a real man." Crew members from other ships told of schemes Bram had suggested on different voyages to kill the captain and steal the ship and its cargo.

The jury found Bram guilty of murder on January 2, 1897, and two months later sentenced him to be hanged. Bram appealed the decision and won a new trial, which resulted in a lesser verdict of life imprisonment. On July 12, 1897, Bram was taken to a federal penitentiary to serve his sentence. There is little question that he would have spent the rest of his days there had it not been for an odd twist of fate.

Mary Roberts Rinehart, a popular novelist and writer of mystery stories, became interested in the Bram case. She used the murder at sea as the plot for her 1914 book, *The After House* ("after house" is another name for chart house). In her version of the story, Westerburg, whom she called Charley Jones, is a homicidal maniac who kills the three victims in a fit of senseless rage.

Theodore Roosevelt, former President of the United States and a loyal fan of Rinehart, read *The After House*. The account convinced him that there had been a terrible miscarriage of justice. He wrote to a number of his influential friends and advised them that Bram was being punished for a crime he hadn't committed.

Another devoted reader of Rinehart was President Woodrow Wilson. Based on his reading of *The After House*, and with the urging of Theodore Roosevelt, President Wilson issued a pardon for Theodore Bram on April 22, 1919.

And there the matter ended. Or did it? Will we ever know the *real* killer? Was Bram guilty? Or was Westerburg the murderer?

Chapter 6

Dr. Crippen

EVERYONE WHO LIVED on Hilldrop Crescent in North London was very well acquainted with Dr. and Mrs. Crippen. The middle-aged physician was small, mild, and bookish, with pink cheeks, thin, light brown hair, and a sandy mustache. Thick, gold-rimmed glasses framed his slightly bulging eyes. His wife, Belle, on the other hand, was big-boned and plump, showy and blustery in manner and voice. Formerly a music hall singer with little talent and even less success, Belle drank heavily and was a shameless flirt.

In his spare time, Dr. Crippen enjoyed puttering in the garden behind their well-kept house. On those occasions Belle usually chose to scold or loudly tongue-lash the gentle man. The neighbors could, of course, clearly hear the woman's nagging and shouting. Many gossiped about the way Dr. Crippen kept calm while she screamed at him.

Early in February 1910 the neighbors began to realize that they no longer saw—or heard—Belle around the house. When asked about her, Dr. Crippen replied that Belle had returned to the United States, the country of her birth, to settle a relative's estate.

Soon it came to the notice of those who lived on the street that a different woman was living at the Crippen

Dr. Crippen.

house. The new arrival, Ethel LeNeve, helped the doctor peddle his patent medicines and promote the various unconventional treatments that he favored.

Not long after Belle's departure, Dr. Crippen was approached by several of her music hall friends to purchase tickets for a charity ball to benefit unemployed performers. Despite the fact that Dr. Crippen always felt terribly out of place with Belle's friends, he agreed to attend, since his wife had helped to organize the event.

Dr. Crippen appeared at the gala with Ethel on his arm. Many were startled to see Dr. Crippen escorting another woman to the ball while his wife was away on a trip. And they were stunned to observe Ethel wearing a pendant that they knew belonged to Belle. Would Belle have gone on a trip to America and left her jewelry at home? Her friends doubted that very much.

Suspecting something amiss, a few people decided to investigate. They contacted the shipping company Belle had sailed with. Curiously, her name did not appear on the passenger list. They surveyed the neighborhood to find someone who had seen Belle packing or leaving the house. No one had witnessed her departure. They pressed Dr. Crippen to give them Belle's address in the United States. He murmured something vague about her traveling from place to place.

Some weeks later Dr. Crippen let it be known that he had received a letter from Belle saying that she had suddenly been taken ill. Soon after that he told of being notified that she had died.

Doubts were growing stronger. Belle's friends kept probing and questioning Dr. Crippen: Where is Belle's body? She was cremated in California, he said. But don't Catholics like Belle prefer burial to cremation? Dr. Crippen shrugged. Could they see the death certificate? Dr. Crippen offered the excuse that he had misplaced it.

By now a number of people were convinced that Belle was the victim of foul play. A small group went to Scotland Yard with their suspicions and the evidence they had gathered.

On July 8, 1910, Chief Inspector Walter Dew paid a call on Dr. Crippen. At first Dr. Crippen kept to his story that Belle had died in America. As Inspector Dew interrogated the unruffled Crippen further, however, the doctor finally admitted that he had lied. He offered to reveal the truth.

Dr. Crippen confessed that he had invented the entire account of Belle's death. In all honesty, he went on to say, he did not know where she was, since she had left him for good, perhaps for someone else. So convincing was the docile Crippen, that Inspector Dew believed him. Nevertheless, he told the doctor it would be necessary to check the details.

By the next day Crippen and Ethel had vanished. Inspector Dew immediately ordered a police search of the Crippen house. The detectives went through the family's living quarters, but found no clues to the mysterious departures. They spent two days digging up the garden Dr. Crippen loved so well. All in vain.

On July 13 they decided to examine the cellar. As Inspector Dew jabbed at the floor of the coal bin with a metal poker, he noticed a loose brick. He raised that brick, and realized that others were loose, too. While he picked up the foundation stones, he was sickened by a revolting stench. So loathsome was the smell that the diggers had to stop their work every few minutes to run outside and gasp fresh air.

Digging in the soil beneath the bricks they unearthed a torso, without head or limbs. On closer examination they found that someone had also removed all the bones from the body. When chemists did their tests they learned that the corpse contained a large amount of hyoscine, a deadly poison. Apparently this was all that was left of the murdered Belle.

For nearly two weeks, investigators had no leads as to the whereabouts of Dr. Crippen and Ethel LeNeve. Then on July 22 Captain Henry Kendall of the S. S. *Montrose*, sailing from England to Canada, wired a message home. Two of the passengers on board his ship resembled newspaper photos of the fugitive couple.

Inspector Dew confirmed that another ship, the S. S. *Laurentic*, was sailing for Canada the next day. It was scheduled to make the crossing in seven days. He booked passage. With luck, he hoped to arrive in Canada before the slower *Montrose*.

The *Laurentic* did dock in Quebec, Canada, first. The *Montrose* pulled in the following day. Inspector Dew boarded the *Montrose* and, led by Captain Kendall, approached a passenger who called himself Mr. Robinson, a merchant.

"Good morning, Dr. Crippen," Inspector Dew said to the stunned man.

As soon as Crippen recognized Dew, a look of resignation crossed his face. After placing him under arrest, the inspector went below deck to find Ethel. She was disguised as a boy, Mr. Robinson's son. Dew took her into custody, too.

At the trial that took place subsequently, more of the background and details of the true story of Crippen came out. Hawley Harvey Crippen, born in Coldwater, Michigan, had earned a medical degree, but preferred selling patent medicines to working as a doctor.

On a visit to New York in 1892 he met and married Kunigunde Mackamotzki, who later adopted the stage name Belle Elmore. Five years later they settled in England, where he opened a London office to sell his concoctions.

From the very start the marriage floundered. Soon Belle began to think of leaving Dr. Crippen. Around the same time, he was making plans to kill her in a perfect crime. Neither one succeeded. She delayed too long and was murdered. He made several blunders and was caught.

The hearing was short. Ethel LeNeve was freed of all charges, but Dr. Crippen was found guilty. The unfortunate man was hanged on November 23, 1910.

Few disputed the fact that he committed the crime and had to pay his debt to society. Still, many felt compassion and pity for the gentle, soft-spoken Crippen. It was said that Dr. Crippen was a kind-hearted man who would never have committed a violent crime without extreme provocation. Slaying Belle was blamed on his disastrous marriage.

There were those, too, who were impressed by Crippen's selfless love for Ethel. While awaiting the hangman, Crippen wrote her a letter that said, "I would have been ready any time and at all times to lay down my life and soul to make you happy." In truth, he did. But unfortunately it involved taking another life.

Chapter 7

Leopold and Loeb: The Crime of the Century

JACOB AND FLORA Franks were worried. It was dinnertime and their son, Bobby, fourteen, was still not home. They knew he planned to remain at school as umpire for a ball game. But the game was surely over by now.

Mr. Franks thought that perhaps the boy had stopped off at the tennis court behind their large, imposing Chicago mansion. He checked, but Bobby wasn't there. They called their son's friends, but everyone said that Bobby had left for home before the game was over.

By nine o'clock on that evening of May 21, 1924, Bobby still had not returned. Could he have been locked in the school building by mistake? Mr. Franks went to search the property.

While he was out, Mrs. Franks got a phone call.

"Your son has been kidnapped," the voice at the other end of the line said. "He is all right. There will be further news in the morning."

With this, the caller hung up. Mrs. Franks crumbled and fell to the floor.

In the middle of the same night, Mr. Franks telephoned the police. Aware that any publicity would scare off the kidnapper, he begged the officer to take the information but do nothing for now.

The following morning a special delivery letter came to the Franks' house. It was from the kidnapper. The instructions were to put $10,000 in old bills in a cigar box and await further orders. It was signed George Johnson. Mr. Franks immediately went to the bank to get the money.

In another part of town at the same time, Tony Mankowski was walking home from his night-shift factory job. As he passed a drainage ditch that ran under a railroad track he saw two bare feet stretched out. A railroad crew came along at that moment. Together they removed the body of a young boy. He was naked. The only sign of personal belongings was a pair of glasses lying on the ground nearby.

A newspaper reporter learned that the body had been found. Having also heard rumors of Bobby Franks' disappearance, he put the two stories together and called the Franks' home. Edwin Gresham, Mr. Franks' brother-in-law agreed to view the body and see if it might be Bobby's.

While Gresham was gone, the phone rang. The man told Mr. Franks that it was George Johnson calling. He told Mr. Franks to go to the drugstore at 1465 East 63rd Street right away to arrange for the return of his son.

No sooner had he hung up than Mr. Franks realized that, in all the excitement, he had forgotten the address. When the phone rang again he prayed it was another call from Johnson. It wasn't. It was Gresham with the tragic news that Bobby was dead.

Meanwhile the phone rang at the drugstore on 63rd Street. A worker picked up the receiver.

"Is Mr. Franks there?" the party asked.

On being told he wasn't, the caller clicked off the line. Somewhat later, the phone sounded again, and the same words were exchanged.

Later that afternoon the Chicago police fully mobilized to find the kidnapper-killer. Hundreds of detectives searched the area where Bobby's body was found. They combed the school grounds where he had umpired the after-school baseball game.

Every possible explanation for the murder was explored. Kidnapped for the ransom and killed by accident? A revenge killing directed against Mr. Franks? The act of a sexual pervert? An accidental death that resulted from some ball players' anger at the umpire?

The police followed through on each lead. They found and questioned witnesses and then booked suspects. But lack of evidence forced the police to release all who were under suspicion.

Doggedly the authorities pressed on. They spoke to a worker in the park near where the body was found. Could he think of anyone who made frequent visits to the park? The attendant recalled a well-dressed young man who often came alone or with classes of young people to watch birds. His name, the worker said, was Nathan Leopold, Jr.

Leopold was summoned for questioning. A brilliant young law student, he was also a very enthusiastic bird-watcher. In reply to a question, Leopold said that he sometimes wore glasses. But police did not even bother to inquire any more about them. They merely asked Leopold to sign a statement detailing his recent visits to the park. As Nathan casually walked out the door, it did not occur to anyone involved in the inquiry that this cocky, privileged man could be responsible for the sordid crime.

Each passing day made the police more frenzied in their pursuit of Bobby Franks' murderer. They made wholesale arrests of drug addicts, sexual perverts, and known criminals. Each one was interrogated; every story was checked.

When all was said and done, there was really only one clue: the eyeglasses found near the body. The officers decided to focus their attention on finding the owner.

The detective located the only Chicago company that sold that particular type of frame. Company clerks checked through fifty thousand sales records. Just three of those frames had left the shops. One had been bought by Nathan Leopold.

The police called on the young man again. This time, though, they insisted on seeing his eyeglasses. Unable to find them anywhere in his house, Leopold finally admitted that they were lost. And he conceded that the found pair belonged to him. Probably he dropped them while bird-watching, he said.

The detectives were not at all convinced. They insisted that Leopold tell more about his activities on the day of the kidnapping and murder.

Now cross and scowling, Leopold said he couldn't remember. Over and over again, the police posed the same questions. Many hours later, Leopold finally agreed to describe the events of May 21.

With his friend Richard Loeb, a student at the University of Chicago, he had eaten lunch. Then, taking flasks of gin and whiskey along, they spent the afternoon bird-watching. Afterward they ate dinner in a restaurant and then went driving. On the way they picked up two girls, Edna and Mae, spent some time with them, and

Richard Loeb (center) and **Nathan Leopold, Jr.** (second from right) during a recess in their trial. Their brothers are seen with them: on the left, Allen and Ernest Loeb, on the extreme right, Foreman Leopold. The two men in the rear are bailiffs. (Wide World Photos)

went home. Leopold claimed that he didn't know the girls' last names, nor could he think of any witnesses who could confirm his story.

It was time now to examine Richard Loeb. Like Leopold, Loeb came from a distinguished, moneyed Chicago family. His father was a vice-president of Sears Roebuck. When called in, he told a story that was basically the same as his friend's.

Some reporters covering the case learned that Leopold belonged to a study group with several other law students. The members typed out "dope sheets" to help them prepare for exams. The reporters obtained copies of some papers that Leopold had typed. Much to their disappointment, they had not been done on the same typewriter as the ransom note.

At that point, though, a group member mentioned that Leopold also owned a portable typewriter. The students located some dope sheets typed on his portable. Experts compared them to the ransom note. Both had been typed on the same machine!

With these findings, the police hurried to the large Leopold house to search for the typewriter. It was nowhere to be seen. The ransom note had been prepared on Leopold's typewriter, but without the machine they had no evidence.

Still, they were making progress. The officials spoke to Leopold's chauffeur about the events on May 21. The driver casually mentioned that he was working on the brakes of Nathan's car that day. This remark was the opening the police were looking for. The two suspects said that they had driven Nathan Leopold's car. It was clear now that they had lied.

The two men, now in separate rooms, were questioned very sharply. At 1:40 A.M. Loeb broke down and confessed to the kidnapping and murder of Bobby Franks. When told that his friend had disclosed all, Leopold confessed, too. That is when the actual story behind the crime of the century emerged.

The two young men, Nathan Leopold, age nineteen, and Richard Loeb, eighteen, had planned the crime for about seven months. Although amply endowed with intelligence, education, and all the advantages of family fortune, they still dreamed of committing the perfect crime. They thought themselves so ingenious that they were certain they would never be caught. In any matching of wits, they felt sure they would come out ahead. The thrill murder they contemplated had no motive other than the sheer excitement of killing someone and getting away with it.

They spent hours mapping every step of the crime. They would kidnap a young boy whose father had enough money to pay a large ransom. The youngster would know one of them slightly to make it easier to lure him into the car. And they would have to kill him, of course, to prevent identification.

The two also decided on a complicated scheme to collect the ransom money after the boy was dead. And, just in case something went wrong, they agreed on the story they would tell of how they spent that fateful day.

On May 21 they rented a car under a false name. Then they drove around the neighborhood looking for a likely victim. Bobby Franks, whom Loeb knew slightly, was walking home alone after leaving the ball game. Loeb invited him into the car. He killed him there by suffocation.

Leopold and Loeb drove off, stripped the body, and dumped the clothes far from the scene of the crime. After dark they drove back to the park and shoved the naked

A crowd of spectators outside the Criminal Courts building in Chicago waiting to be admitted to the Leopold-Loeb trial. (Wide World Photos)

corpse into the drainage ditch. That is when Leopold's glasses fell out of his jacket pocket—the accident that was to doom them.

All the world watched and read the details of the cold-blooded kidnap-murder, committed for thrills and the challenge of beating the system. Both men were found guilty and sentenced to life in prison.

Neither, though, served his full sentence. Loeb died in a prison brawl in 1936, and Leopold was paroled in 1958. After his release, Leopold married. He died in 1971 at the age of sixty-six.

Chapter 8

The Murder Gang: Five Frustrated Killers

LATE IN 1931 a gang of five young men in the Bronx, New York—Tony Marino, Joe Murphy, Dan Kreisberg, Harry Green, and Frank Pasqua—came up with what they thought was a foolproof scheme to strike it rich. They took out a life insurance policy on Michael Malloy, a local drunkard. Since Malloy was almost always under the influence of alcohol, they were sure it would be easy to do him in.

The gang pondered the many possible ways to do the deed. Since Malloy was such a heavy drinker, they finally decided to poison his liquor. Malloy was a nightly customer at Marino's speakeasy, so this was easily arranged.

Marino offered Malloy free drinks for the evening. He set them out, one after another, all doctored with such poisons as turpentine, wood alcohol, and horse liniment. Malloy was delighted. He belted down many glassfuls of the deadly, foul-tasting concoctions and asked for more. The gang members watched in disbelief as Malloy did not even get sick.

Later that night, after giving up efforts to poison

Malloy, Harry Green, a taxi driver, volunteered to run him over. As Malloy was staggering home, Green hit him with his cab. Sure that the car had accomplished what the poisons had not, Green left Malloy lying in the middle of the street. Proud of their achievement, the gang of five went home to sleep and dream of the insurance money they would collect.

During the night, Malloy was found. He was taken to a hospital, treated for his injuries, and released.

After Malloy returned to the neighborhood, his "friends" invited him to a party to celebrate the return of his good health. At the gathering they offered him a sardine sandwich. Mixed in with the fish, though, were a number of tiny carpet tacks. If Malloy thought the sandwich tasted strange, he did not say so. In fact, after finishing, he just popped another into his mouth. And the two sandwiches of sardines studded with tacks didn't even give him a stomach ache!

Just when the would-be killers were beginning to think they were never going to succeed, they came up with still another plan. The next night, with the temperature below zero and the ground covered with snow, the fearsome five gave Malloy enough drinks to get him completely drunk. In this state they took him to the Bronx Zoo. Once there they stripped him of his clothes and soaked him with several buckets of cold water. Then they left, absolutely sure that now they would only have to wait until morning when Malloy's frozen corpse would be found.

The gang met early the next day at Marino's bar. But instead of the expected news of Malloy's death, in walked Malloy himself!

"I sure need a drink," Malloy said to Marino. "Somehow I've caught this god-awful head cold."

The five looked at one another in shock and amazement. They resolved to change their tactics. Maybe they'd been nice guys for too long.

This time, they again gave him as much liquor as he wanted, especially as he now needed it to treat his cold. When he had nearly passed out, they took him to a room they had rented. They attached one end of a rubber hose to the tap of the gaslight. The other end they placed in Malloy's mouth. Then they turned on the gas and left.

On the following day poor Malloy was found—dead. The five gang members collected the insurance money and divided it.

Their satisfaction was short-lived, though. The police began speaking to the neighborhood people. Harry Green offered to confess if he was granted immunity. The district attorney agreed, and Green described their four failures at murder and told how they finally succeeded.

Helped by this admission of guilt, the others were brought to trail and found guilty of killing Michael Malloy. They were sentenced to die. All four were executed in the electric chair at Sing Sing prison in Ossining, New York.

Chapter 9

Nannie Doss: A Romantic at Heart

IF YOU HAD seen Nannie Doss on the streets of Tulsa, Oklahoma, between 1940 and 1950, you probably would not have given her a second glance. Unattractive, plump, and dressed very plainly, she had little to make her stand out from the crowd.

Yet, in Nannie's dreams she was beautiful and accomplished, ready to be swept off her feet by a rich, exciting, and handsome lover who would clasp her in his powerful but gentle arms.

Each month Nannie eagerly read every word in her favorite magazine, *True Romance*. How she yearned for the torrid kisses and passionate embraces enjoyed by the good-looking, rich, successful heroines on whom fortune always seemed to smile.

Like Nannie, many people lead lives that are very dull compared with those of the fictional lovers that they read about. Most understand that reality seldom equals the extravagance of make-believe. Not Nannie. She had visions and dreams of love and romance that she wanted, and expected, in her own life.

The Nannie Doss story came to light in October

1954 after the middle-aged woman brought her husband Samuel to the hospital suffering with sharp, powerful stomach pains. The doctors could not immediately determine the cause. The next day he was dead.

Hospital officials, eager to identify the cause of Samuel's death, asked Nannie's permission to perform an autopsy. She readily agreed, saying, "Whatever he had might kill somebody else. It's best to find out."

The results shocked and dismayed everyone. Samuel Doss had been poisoned. His body contained enough arsenic to kill, not one, but twenty healthy men!

A squad car was sent to pick up Nannie. When the police notified her of the autopsy findings, Nannie just clucked her tongue and shook her head in disbelief.

"I don't understand it," she said in her soft, gentle way. "How could such a thing happen? All I fed him when he came home was a dish of stewed prunes, and there was certainly no arsenic in that."

Nannie accompanied the police to headquarters. She proved to be a willing but forgetful witness. Smiling and giggling like a teenager through the many hours of questioning, Nannie tried to give the officers all the information they wanted. But there was one major problem. She seemed to have great difficulty remembering much of what had happened.

Things reached a climax when police asked her about Richard Morton, her fourth husband, the one who had preceded Samuel Doss.

"I have never heard of any Richard Morton," she countered.

"What?" the detective exclaimed. "You don't remember your previous husband?"

"Oh, *that* Richard Morton," Nannie coyly replied.

As detectives stepped up their investigation, day by

day, hour after hour, Doss managed to remember some very surprising details. Among the most startling was the fact that she had not only poisoned her fifth husband but had also killed the fourth.

With this confession, police set out to get an exact count of how many poor souls had enjoyed Nannie's stewed prunes laced with arsenic before they died. They obtained orders to dig up the bodies of relatives who had expired under suspicious circumstances. The results, together with Nannie's testimony at the trial, revealed some shocking information about this lady's incredible life.

Nannie's first husband was the only one of the five men she married who was still living at the time of the trial. Before their divorce, they had three children. She murdered two of the children with arsenic. The third survived.

The four husbands who perished all endured stomach pains before expiring of huge doses of the same poison. Among the relatives, Nannie had served prunes or some other arsenic-flavored dish to her mother, two of her sisters, a nephew, and a grandson. The staggering total came to eleven known murders!

The judge tried to discover Nannie's motive. Did she murder for the insurance money? Nannie was deeply insulted. Although she did get some small sums, it was not the thought of money that made her plot the killings, she insisted.

Then why did she kill? The real reason, Nannie explained, was that she was seeking the perfect mate, "the real romance of life." She wanted to be married to one who would make her life as rich and exciting as those she read about in *True Romance*. As each man in turn failed to live up to her hopes and expectations, she needed to kill him so she would be free to marry Mr. Right when he came along.

One more mystery remained. Why had she poisoned her mother, children, and sisters? Nannie had no answer. She merely shrugged and kept quiet.

Given a life sentence, Nannie Doss died in prison at the age of sixty. To the end, she read and reread her favorite love stories and dreamed of heroes and heroines leading ideal lives in a fictional paradise.

Chapter 10

Albert DeSalvo: The Boston Strangler

It BEGAN IN Boston during 1960. A handsome man—twenty-nine years old, married, with two young children—named Albert DeSalvo launched a career in crime that resulted in his own death at Walpole State Prison, Massachusetts, thirteen years later.

DeSalvo's first escapades involved gaining entrance to the apartments of women living alone in the Boston area. His method was to knock on a number of doors, which he chose at random. If a man answered, he said it was a mistake. If a woman came to the door and appeared to be single, he explained that he was from a modeling agency. He had heard that she had a good face and figure. The agency had sent him to take her measurements and arrange for a contract.

A few girls refused to let DeSalvo enter. Most, though, excited by the prospect of a glamorous career in fashion, opened the door. They posed and allowed him to assess parts of their bodies. Some even offered to undress in order to help him get their exact dimensions. A few urged him to stay and visit with them.

There was, of course, no model agency. But for over a year the Measuring Man, as DeSalvo came to be called, carried on his racket without interference. Then, on March 17, 1961, the police picked him up for carrying burglary tools, even though he had never used them.

A few of the women he had deceived recognized DeSalvo as the Measuring Man. They pressed charges, and DeSalvo served eleven months in prison. He was released in April 1962.

Scarcely two months later, DeSalvo told his wife that he was going fishing. But instead of driving to the shore, he headed into Boston. After parking the car, he chose the first house and the first apartment that caught his eye. It happened to be apartment 3F at 77 Gainsborough Street. When he knocked, fifty-five-year-old Anna Slesers opened the door.

"I was sent to do some work in your bathroom," DeSalvo announced.

She let him in. As Anna led the way through the apartment, DeSalvo struck her a crushing blow on the head with a heavy lead weight. The poor woman fell to the floor dead. He took the belt from her robe and tied it tightly around her neck. He stole nothing and, aside from turning off the phonograph that had been playing while he was there, he didn't even touch anything.

Two weeks later DeSalvo chose an address not far from Anna Slesers' house. Mary Mullen, age eighty-five, let him in after he told her, "I got to do some work in the apartment."

Once inside, they sat and talked for a few minutes. Then she got up. DeSalvo lunged and grabbed her around the neck with his powerful right arm. In an instant her body grew limp, and she slumped to the floor. He lifted her dead form and placed it on a couch. As he casually strolled out of the building and back to his car, he even waved to a policeman on the beat.

Helen Blake, age sixty-five, was next. On the morn-

Albert DeSalvo was wearing a navy uniform when he was captured by police in Lynn, Massachusetts, north of Boston. (Wide World Photos)

ing of June 30 DeSalvo got into her apartment as he had with the others. He choked her with his arm. The woman passed out but didn't die. So DeSalvo tied one of her stockings around her neck and choked her to death.

Just six hours later, DeSalvo was in the apartment of sixty-eight-year-old Nina Nichols. The story was as grisly as before. This time, though, he tried to strangle her with a belt. But he pulled it so tight that the buckle tore off. He snatched a stocking from her dresser, wrapped it around her neck, and tugged on it with all his strength. She soon stopped breathing.

By now the entire city of Boston was in a panic. Some say the newspapers fanned the fears that already gripped the city by calling the unknown killer the Boston Strangler. Women of all ages locked themselves inside their homes. The public clamored for the police to find the maniac who seemed to be killing women without reason or motive.

Many known criminals were hauled in for police questioning, and as often happens, some made false confessions. But the experts couldn't pin this rash of senseless murders on any one individual they interviewed.

DeSalvo lay low during July. But in August two more elderly females fell prey to his vicious attacks—Ida Irga, age seventy-five, and Jane Sullivan, age sixty-seven.

No more slayings were reported for the following three months. But on December 5, the date of his wedding anniversary, DeSalvo was again on the prowl. This time, though, he struck and assaulted a young woman, twenty-year-old Sophie Clark. She became another victim.

The Boston Strangler killings continued through 1963 and into early 1964. Four more innocent sufferers were young, like Sophie Clark. Two of the other unfortunate victims were elderly, like the first ones to fall to DeSalvo's wrath.

A long period of watchful waiting, about nine months, ended on October 27, 1964, when the strangler attacked once more. But this time, instead of gaining entry by posing as a repairman, he actually broke into the apartment. Inside he found a twenty-year-old college student. He forced her down on the bed and, holding a knife to her throat, gagged and tied her up.

After assaulting her, DeSalvo unexpectedly said, "I'm sorry," and left abruptly.

As soon as the girl freed herself she called the authorities and gave a full description of her attacker to a police artist, who drew a sketch. From the picture, a detective spotted the resemblance to Albert DeSalvo, the Measuring Man.

The police picked DeSalvo up for questioning. While he was at headquarters, details of his appearance went out to other police departments. Reports came in from elsewhere in Massachusetts as well as from Connecticut, New Hampshire, and Rhode Island. A man who fit DeSalvo's description had assaulted over three hundred women in these states over a period of about four years!

While he was being detained, the investigators learned of even more crimes that he had committed. Albert DeSalvo was the Boston Strangler. He confessed to killing thirteen women. Police could only guess at how many more he had slain or raped during the years he followed his dreadful calling.

In 1966 DeSalvo was committed to Boston State Hospital, a mental institution. The following year he was tried in court and sentenced to a life term in prison. Seven years later the Boston Strangler was found dead in his jail cell, stabbed by a fellow inmate.

11

Richard Speck: "Born to Raise Hell"

RICHARD SPECK, A semiliterate drifter, worked irregularly as a sailor aboard various cargo ships. At the end of June 1966 Speck was fired from his job on a freighter after a row with a ship's officer. On July 10 the unemployed seaman appeared in the union hiring hall in Chicago to get work on a vessel going to New Orleans. All jobs were taken.

For the next few days Speck hung around bars, drinking heavily and taking drugs. On the night of July 13, drunk and befuddled, Speck walked the streets of Chicago's South Side, near the hiring hall. After a while he stopped in front of a residence for student nurses at South Chicago Community Hospital and decided to enter.

Corazon Amurao, twenty-three years old, answered his knock on the door. Reeking of alcohol and brandishing a knife and a gun, Speck forced his way past her and into the house.

"I'm not going to hurt you," he said. "I need your money to go to New Orleans."

With a wave of his gun, Speck ordered Miss Amurao

and two other girls into an upstairs bedroom where three others were already present. He made the six young women lie face down on the floor. As three more student nurses returned home, Speck forced them to get down, too. He bound all nine hand and foot with strips that he tore from a bed sheet.

For the following half-hour the intruder went through the house looking for money and pocketing whatever he found. Then he came back to the room where his captives lay on the floor.

Speck played with his gun nervously for a while and then seemed to reach a decision. He untied the feet of one woman, who was only twenty years of age, and led her out of the room. Moments later there was a deep gasp. Then silence.

After about twenty minutes Speck returned alone. He untied two more girls and took them to a different bedroom. Another long interval passed, and Speck came back for still another victim. And then another and another.

Meanwhile, Corazon Amurao, though she was tied up, managed to roll over, slide under a bed, and wedge herself tightly against the wall, out of the killer's sight. From her hiding place, the terrified Amurao saw Speck's devilish moves. At last he did not reappear any more. Probably he lost count of the girls. In any event, he didn't look for Amurao.

At about 5:30 A.M. Miss Amurao decided that Speck had left for good. She wriggled along the floor and struggled to free herself of the cloth strips that bound her. As she started down the hall she saw, extending out from the bathroom, a pair of girl's feet. She realized that the girl was dead, and she soon discovered that her other friends were dead, too.

Barely able to look at the cruelly abused bodies lying around like broken, twisted dolls, Miss Amurao made her way to a window that faced the street. She kicked out the screen, squirmed through the opening, and screamed for help.

The police arrived quickly. Of the eight victims, three had been stabbed to death, three more had died from a combination of stabbing and strangulation, and two had been strangled. The killer's fingerprints were found in more than thirty places.

The search for the mass murderer started at once. Miss Amurao, when she recovered from shock, gave a very complete description of the tall, blond, pock-marked attacker. A police artist made a sketch that appeared in all of the Chicago newspapers. Two detectives noted that the well-made square knots used to bind the nurses were the kind a sailor might use. And they observed that the nurses' hands were tied with their palms facing outward, the way police handcuff dangerous prisoners, indicating the murderer had probably served time.

With the fingerprints, the drawing, and other clues, police fanned out through the neighborhood. A gas station worker recalled that a man matching that description said he was staying at the Ship Yard Inn. The police officers hurried over, but Speck had already checked out.

At the hiring hall for sailors, just half a block from where the carnage had occurred, an agent remembered the face in the drawing. A man who looked like that had been trying to get a job on any ship going to New Orleans. When his application was found, the name on it was Richard Speck. The fingerprints found at the scene of the crimes matched those in Speck's police record, which was in the FBI files.

The police found many more witnesses who had seen or spoken to Speck in the days before the dastardly murders. One woman told of a tattoo on Speck's left arm: "Born to Raise Hell."

The police stepped up the manhunt. The newspapers continued to publish Speck's description in the hope that someone would spot him and call the authorities. Stakeouts were posted around the city in an attempt to nab him.

Yet, by Saturday night, three days after the slayings, Speck was still at large. About midnight on July 16, 1966, a report came in that a man staying at a 90¢-a-night skid-row hotel had slashed his wrists. An ambulance rushed over and took the attempted-suicide victim, who said his name was B. Brian, to Cook County Hospital.

Dr. Leroy Smith in the emergency room started to clean the wounds. He wiped away the blood that covered Brian's arms. Slowly the tattoo on the left arm became visible. When the arm was free of blood, the words could easily be read: "Born to Raise Hell."

Recalling the description of the nurse killer he had read in the newspaper, Dr. Smith asked, "What's your name?"

"Richard. Richard Speck."

The following spring, it took the jury less than an hour to find Speck guilty of all eight murders. Sentenced to die in the electric chair, his life was spared by the Supreme Court's abolition of capital punishment. Speck was later resentenced to a prison term of four hundred years—fifty years for each of the lives he had so callously snuffed out.

Chapter 12

Charles Manson: Helter-Skelter

THE EARLY LIFE of Charles Manson gave little indication of his later power to control the minds and actions of others. It did sow the seeds, however, for some of the most wicked crimes in recent times.

Manson was born in Cincinnati, Ohio, on November 12, 1934, to a teenage prostitute. By the age of five he was living with an aunt while his mother served a five-year prison term for armed robbery. Paroled three years later, his mother dragged him through a succession of run-down hotels and rooming houses. When he was twelve years old, his mother abandoned Manson, forcing him to make his way alone in the world.

Turning to crime to support himself, Manson spent the next twenty years in and out of jail—but mostly in. On March 21, 1967, his release date, he asked to be allowed to remain in prison. Having spent seventeen of his thirty-two years behind bars, he feared he could not adjust to life as a free man. But the prison system had no room for him, and he was discharged.

Manson settled first in the Haight-Ashbury section of San Francisco, a center of hippie culture in the 1960s.

Charles Manson.
(Wide World Photos)

"Hippie" is a term used to describe young people during the 1960s who rejected the life-style and various ideas of conventional society. Many hippies lived in groups and communes and used drugs. A good number followed a mystical leader or guru.

Feeling comfortable in the hippie culture, Manson moved in with a thirty-two-year-old librarian named Mary Brunner. After a while another woman came to live with them. Before too long, eight people were living in one house. With the exception of Manson and Brunner, all were in their teens or early twenties. They were all fascinated by the ex-convict, with his strange philosophy that was a blend of mysticism, fear, and love. They called themselves "the family" and Manson was their unquestioned leader.

With money they obtained, mostly from begging, Manson bought an old school bus, took out the seats, and created a mobile home. For about a year and a half the "family" drove around California and other states in the West. Finally they settled at Spahn Ranch on the outskirts of Los Angeles. The ranch had been the setting for many old Hollywood westerns. By now the buildings and grounds were run down. The aged, nearly blind owner of the property was barely aware that the Manson family had moved into the empty movie sets.

While the Manson family lived at Spahn Ranch, it numbered between twenty-five and thirty members. Most were young girls, some no more than thirteen or fourteen years old, and the group had a ratio of five females to every male. The short, bearded Manson was a strong, authoritative father figure for the group. A stare from his deep, dark eyes was usually enough to impose his will on any of the family members. They regarded him as a Christ-like figure and were ready to carry out his orders without hesitation.

Manson played guitar and wrote songs, but he was unsuccessful in getting the recording contract he sought. For money, the family members stole automobiles and whatever else they could get their hands on. For food, they went on "garbage runs," collecting scraps of food that were thrown out by restaurants.

In his preachings to the family, Manson menacingly predicted a horrific clash between blacks and whites, which he called Helter-Skelter. Helter-Skelter was to be the first step in the mad scheme that Manson was hatching for world domination.

Charles Manson's plan for starting the Helter-Skelter was to commit some particularly hideous, motiveless murders of white people. He had two purposes in mind: first to instill fear in the whites, and second to show blacks, by example, how to terrorize and conquer the white population.

Manson believed his strategy would unleash great chaos and precipitate a bloody war between blacks and whites in which the blacks would triumph. Amid the resultant turmoil Manson's family would escape to the desert where they would grow and multiply until they reached 144,000 souls, a figure he took from the Bible. The number represented twelve tribes of 12,000 each.

Once the blacks had won control, Manson proposed to make his move. He would lead his followers back from the desert. Their great might would overcome the black leadership, and Manson would become the divine ruler of all.

On the afternoon of Friday, August 8, 1969, Manson announced to the family, "Now's the time for Helter-Skelter." After dinner he called aside four members: Tex (Charles Watson, age twenty-three), Sadie (Susan Atkins, twenty-one), Katie (Patricia Krenwinkel, twenty-one), and Linda (Linda Kasabian, twenty-one). He told each to get a knife and to "do what Tex tells you." They hid the knives and Tex's gun beneath the car seat. As they drove off, Manson stopped the car, leaned in, and said, "Leave a sign. You girls know what to write. Something witchy."

At about midnight they parked the car at the driveway entrance to a large, luxurious, isolated house at 10050 Cielo Drive near Benedict Canyon, Los Angeles. Tex got out, climbed the telephone pole, and cut the wire.

Just then a car went by. Tex stopped it and threatened the driver, Steven Parent, age eighteen, a delivery boy for a plumbing company.

"Please don't hurt me," the terrified young man cried. "I won't say anything."

Four shots rang out in the still, hot August night. Tex called the girls, and together they pushed Parent's car with its grim cargo up the driveway and left it there.

Tex then broke into the huge house on Cielo Drive by crawling through a window. He admitted Sadie and Katie, who checked all the rooms. They found four people at home: Sharon Tate, age twenty-six, movie star and wife of Roman Polanski, the film director, eight and a half months pregnant; Jay Sebring, thirty-five, world famous hair stylist; Abigail Folger, twenty-five, wealthy coffee heiress; and Voytek Frykowski, thirty-two, playboy lover of Abigail.

Voytek Frykowski was asleep on the living room couch. Tex woke him and ordered Sadie to tie him up.

"Who are you?" the alarmed Voytek asked.

"I am the devil, and I have come to do the devil's work," replied Tex.

Katie and Sadie now brought the others into the living room at knifepoint. All three were told to lie face down. When Sebring objected, Tex shot him and Sebring fell. Tex then tied a rope around the wounded man's neck and around the necks of Abigail and Sharon. He threw the end of the rope over a ceiling beam and started pulling on it. The two women had to stand up to avoid being choked to death.

On Tex's orders, Sadie stabbed Frykowski four or five times before he freed himself and ran screaming to the door. Tex chased him, beating his head with the gun butt and then stabbing and shooting Frykowski. The victim's body showed two bullet wounds, thirteen blows to the head, and fifty-one stab wounds.

While this was going on, Tex heard Sebring moaning. He ran over to the hurt man and stabbed him viciously in the back seven times. Abigail Folger got twenty-eight stab injuries from Katie. And Sadie killed Sharon with sixteen blows with a knife.

"I just kept stabbing her until she stopped screaming" was her matter-of-fact statement.

Remembering Manson's order to leave a message, Sadie picked up a towel, dipped it into the blood flowing from Sharon Tate, and wrote "Pig" on the door. Then the four killers left the house. They were back at the ranch by about 2:00 A.M.

The following night, after dinner, Manson again called his family together. He announced that it was time for another killing spree. This time Manson himself got into the driver's seat of the car. In addition to the four from the last night's murders, Leslie (Leslie Van Houton, age twenty) and Clem (Steve Grogan, seventeen) also went along.

For some time they just cruised around seeking a house for their murderous Helter-Skelter. At one residence Manson got out, looked in the window, and returned to the car because he saw pictures of children and decided not to "do" the house. In the same impulsive way Manson stopped at a church, but finding the door locked, decided to keep going. At last the group arrived at 3301 Waverly Drive in the Los Feliz section of Los Angeles. There was no turning away now.

Manson went into the house alone. After ten minutes he came out and said he had tied up the man and woman he found inside. He commanded Tex, Katie, and Leslie to go in and kill them. After the executions they were "to paint a picture more gruesome than anybody had ever seen." When they were finished, they were to hitchhike to the ranch. With the instructions given, Manson and the others left for home.

The three who remained prepared to carry out the murderous charge. Katie and Leslie brought the woman, Rosemary LaBianca, age thirty-eight, into the bedroom. The two knifed her to death with forty-one wounds, thirty-six in her back. Tex stayed in the living room with the man, Leno LaBianca, forty-four. He killed Leno by inflicting twelve fatal stab wounds.

Using Leno LaBianca's blood, they wrote the words "Death to pigs" and "Rise" on the living room walls. On the refrigerator door they scrawled the Manson motto— "Helter-Skelter."

Then Katie entered the living room with a large fork, the kind used to hold meat or poultry while it is being carved. She stabbed Leno fourteen more times. To end the task, she carved the word "war" across his stomach.

The two nights of murder gripped the entire city of Los Angeles in terror. Neither crime seemed to be motivated by robbery or revenge. Nor did it spark the revolt of blacks against whites that Manson had hoped for.

There appeared to be no leads and no suspects in the brutal, senseless slayings. Even when Manson and some family members were arrested and sentenced to prison in October for auto theft, the authorities had no suspicion that they were the cold-blooded murderers.

The evidence against Manson started to mount after Sadie boasted to her jail-mates of her crimes. Linda then testified that Manson and the family were responsible for the Tate and LaBianca murders as well as a number of others. Manson was brought to trial on June 15, 1970, along with his followers, Susan "Sadie" Atkins, Patricia "Katie" Krenwinkel, and Leslie Van Houten. Charles "Tex" Watson was tried later. All were charged with murder.

The highly publicized trial went on for nine months before the verdict of guilty and the sentence of death came in. When California abolished the death penalty on February 18, 1972, the terms were changed to life imprisonment. Of the man still serving his time in prison, the prosecutor said that Manson was "one of the most evil, satanic men who ever walked the face of the earth."

Chapter 13

Peter Sutcliffe: The Yorkshire Ripper

THE FIRST VICTIM was Anna Rogelsky, age thirty-four, from the small town of Keighley, in the English county of Yorkshire. On Friday, July 4, 1975, Anna took a bus to the nearby city of Bradford to spend the evening drinking at Bibby's Club. She returned home around 1:00 A.M. and then walked across town to visit her boyfriend. He was not at home. A short while later her fully clothed body was found in an alley behind a movie theater. Nothing had been taken from her pocketbook. The cause of death was three brutal blows to the back of the head. A number of strange marks had been slashed into the skin on her abdomen.

The next incident, six weeks later, was similar. Olive Smelt, age forty-six, also of Yorksire, was spending Friday night in her usual way. First she met her friends for drinks. Then she picked up some fish and chips to take home for a late supper. At fifteen minutes before midnight, as Olive was taking a shortcut through an alley to the fish-and-chips shop, a man came alongside her. She noticed his dark hair and beard. He said something about the weather, and then she felt a crashing blow to the back of her head. Olive dragged herself to a nearby house and was taken to the hospital. Here the doctors also found two eight-inch cuts on her back. Again, no hint of robbery.

The third person to be found suffered an even more chilling beating and stabbing. Wilomena McCann, age twenty-eight, lived in the city of Leeds. On October 29 she put her nine-year-old son in charge of the younger children and went out for some drinking and dancing in the pubs, and perhaps to spend the night with a man for money. Wilomena was seen leaving the pub alone at 10:30 P.M.

At 7:41 the next morning a milkman saw a soft heap under an overcoat near the Prince Philip Playing Fields. Wilomena was lying dead with her clothes pulled back, exposing her naked body. She had been dealt two severe blows to the back of the head with a hammerlike object, followed by fifteen stab wounds to the neck, chest, and stomach.

Six more murders followed this grisly pattern. The victims were all woman who were often seen in cheap pubs and dancing clubs in western Yorkshire county. They were believed to be prostitutes. Death came as a result of hammer blows to the head and knife or screwdriver slashes and stabs to the body. No signs of rape or robbery were apparent.

The police guessed that these clearly related crimes were the work of one crazed killer. A sensational headline in the *Yorkshire Post* early in 1976 compared these sinister killings with those of Jack the Ripper, the murderer of prostitutes a hundred years earlier (see Chapter 3). It called the unknown killer the Yorkshire Ripper. The name caught on.

On the evening of June 25, 1976, the Yorkshire Ripper struck again. This time his target was not a prostitute

Peter Sutciffe, the Yorkshire Ripper. (Wide World Photos)

but sixteen-year-old Jayne Macdonald, who worked in a local supermarket. Jayne had been out for an evening of dancing with her friends. Early Sunday morning her body was discovered. It showed the Ripper's telltale signature: hammer blows on the head, multiple stab wounds on the body, and disarranged clothes.

With teenager Jayne's murder, the anger of the British public erupted into fierce outrage. The police, already showing the strain of the inquiry, doubled their efforts.

One precious bit of evidence that they had was a distinctive tire pattern found in the ground near one victim's body. The tires on about 100,000 cars in England had that pattern. Detectives were checking as many of those cars as possible.

Then imprints of a boot were found on two of the bodies. Perhaps the marks had been made by the Yorkshire Ripper as he kicked and trampled the women in a fit of fury. It proved to be a very popular brand of boot. Tracing it was just about impossible. Of special interest, though, was a worn spot on the right sole. It showed that the owner drove for a living, since the spot was probably caused by pressing with that foot on a gas pedal for several hours every day.

One of the Yorkshire Ripper's victims had a brand-new five-pound note in her purse. Could the killer have given her the money? A member of the Yorkshire Ripper super squad learned that similar new notes had been in the pay envelopes received by some eight thousand workers in Yorkshire. The police undertook the staggering job of interviewing all of these people to find a possible suspect. They were unable, though, to connect anyone with the slayings. And the slaughter continued, one murder more savage than the last.

The assault on Theresa Sykes, age sixteen, followed. The big difference here was that Theresa was able to escape. She proved to be a key witness in the investigation.

Theresa was on her way home across a field from a grocery shop at eight o'clock on the evening of November 5, 1980, when she received a stunning blow to the back of her head. As she fell, she saw a bearded man about to strike her again. Her desperate screams drove the attacker off and brought a neighbor to Theresa's aid. Though she lived to tell her story, the woman will have to bear a half-moon-shaped scar etched into her forehead forever.

By the end of 1980 the Yorkshire Ripper had brutally murdered thirteen women. Another seven had been marred for life by assaults that they survived. Over the nearly five years of investigation, officers and detectives quizzed nearly 200,000 suspects and witnesses, placed extra patrols on the streets, set up decoys in the seedy districts of several Yorkshire cities, and checked the

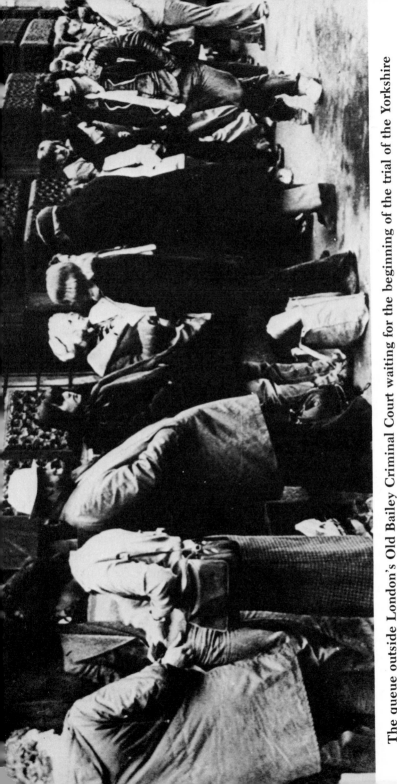

The queue outside London's Old Bailey Criminal Court waiting for the beginning of the trial of the Yorkshire Ripper. (Wide World Photos)

drivers of thousands of cars. And they were still far from a solution.

The arrest, when it did come, happened quite unexpectedly. On January 2, 1981, police officers Robert Ring and Robert Hydes were cruising along quiet, deserted Melbourne Avenue in the city of Sheffield, Yorkshire. It was a favorite area for men to pick up prostitutes. The officers spotted a parked car with a couple inside. They recognized the woman, Olivia Reivers, a convicted prostitute. The man gave his name as Peter Williams.

Through the computer terminal mounted in the patrol car, the men checked his car's registration plates. The message that flashed back showed that they were stolen plates. The policemen took the couple to the station house for questioning.

Olivia Reivers was released in short order, but Peter Williams was held on the stolen-plate charge. Because of a possible connection with the Yorkshire Ripper case, police were sent to search the area where the arrest had been made. They did indeed find a hammer and knife like those thought to be used in several of the slayings.

Peter Williams Sutcliffe, as his real name proved to be, calmly denied that he was the Yorkshire Ripper or that he was involved in any of the murders. The questioning kept on, though. It turned to the night of November 5 and the attack on Theresa Sykes. Sutcliffe maintained that he arrived home from work that night at eight o'clock. By now, however, Sutcliffe's wife was being interviewed separately. She said he had returned at ten.

As police continued the interrogation, point by point, Sutcliffe suddenly said, "I think you are leading up to the Yorkshire Ripper."

"What about the Yorkshire Ripper?" Detective John Boyle asked.

"Well, that's me."

As the team checked back over the long inquiry, they found that they had questioned Sutcliffe nine times over the years. His relaxed, quiet manner and his apparently happy marriage had made them dismiss him time after time. Also, officers had received a tape recording from someone who claimed to be the Yorkshire Ripper. Sutcliffe did not sound like the voice on the tape, so he was let go for that reason as well.

People who knew Sutcliffe were shocked and dismayed to think that he would unleash so horrid a wave of terror. As is often the case, experts looked to his childhood and youth for some explanation.

Born June 2, 1946, Peter had been weak, small, and shy as a lad. On entering his teens he started body-building exercises, becoming very strong and powerful. In the years when many young men start to notice girls, Peter's only real interest was in motorbikes. Perhaps most important of all, throughout his growing-up years Peter kept up an excessive and extraordinary attachment to his mother.

Soon after leaving school, Sutcliffe got a job as a gravedigger in the local cemetery. Known to the other workers as Jesus, because of his neatly trimmed beard, Peter was said to delight in cracking macabre jokes about the dead.

As a young man of twenty Sutcliffe frequently went drinking at the local pubs, but he never so much as looked at the girls, as his friends did. At this time, though, he met his first and only girl friend, Sonia Szurma. About eight years later, on August 10, 1974, they were married.

In time, Peter left the cemetery job and became a truck driver, a job that he held until his capture. The couple also bought a modest house. While they were not overly friendly with neighbors, they did keep in close touch with their families. Over the years Sonia suffered three miscarriages and was finally told by doctors that she would never be able to bear a child.

In seeking the reason for Sutcliffe's extreme violence, the police asked if Sonia's inability to have children had inspired the vicious slayings of other women. Not at all, replied Sutcliffe, before giving his explanation for the killings.

One woman, he explained, had been nasty and rude to him and had said he was not good. Another wore perfume that was cheap-smelling and too strong. He killed two who were not prostitutes merely to throw the police off the trail. He struck one female because she was wearing tight yellow jeans. And he assaulted his last victim, Theresa Sykes, because she wore a skirt with a slit in the side.

The trial at the famous Old Bailey courthouse in London lasted two weeks. Sutcliffe's defense was that Jesus had spoken to him in the cemetery, ordering him to kill prostitutes and any women who looked even slightly disreputable.

After six hours of deliberation, the jury found Sutcliffe guilty and committed him to life in prison.

Chapter 14

David Berkowitz: Son of Sam

OPERATION OMEGA WAS the single biggest manhunt in the history of the New York Police Department. At its peak, three hundred detectives were working full-time to find a killer who struck often and called himself Son of Sam. Experts tracked down every lead. Decoys were stationed around the metropolitan area in unmarked cars. Autos were stopped and searched at entrances to bridges and tunnels. Over three thousand suspects were arrested and questioned during the long search. It took nearly a full year of dogged police effort to end the nightmare and put Son of Sam behind bars.

The investigators had a few clues to work with. In each attack the killer chose the victim, the time, and the place by chance, in a random way. The chief weapon used in most of the assaults was a .44-caliber pistol. The crimes occurred at night; the victims were young, usually female. Always the murderer appeared suddenly, crouched, fired, and left the scene without robbing or molesting his prey in any other way.

The series of ugly murders began on Christmas Eve, 1975. That night Son of Sam, who lived in Yonkers, New

York, just north of New York City, tucked a hunting knife into his belt. He got into his Ford Galaxie and started to drive aimlessly. His mission was to satisfy the persistent demons that he heard in his mind. They were now ordering him to kill young women.

The crazed Son of Sam drove on, little caring where he was going. At one point he passed a supermarket. A young woman was coming out carrying a bag of groceries. He slowed down. He heard the devil's voice scream, "Get her, get her!" He pulled over and climbed out of the car. Heavy-set and slow moving, he trailed after her.

The voices in his head grew harsher. "She has to be sacrificed!" they seemed to shriek. He raised the knife and plunged it deep into her back. Then he lifted it again and drove it even more deeply into her body.

The woman turned and cried out. Shocked and frightened by the grotesque attacker, she yelled as loudly as she could while fighting and struggling. Later Son of Sam said of this victim, "She was screaming pitifully. I didn't know what the hell to do. It wasn't like the movies. In the movies you sneak up on someone and they fall down quietly." In a panic Son of Sam turned and fled. The woman's wails continued to echo in the crisp night air.

Soon Son of Sam stopped running. Gasping for breath, he leaned on a wire fence. He had failed. The demons had commanded him to kill, and he had missed the mark. He felt weak and fearful.

Looking up and down the empty streets, he tried to spot another person to sacrifice. Someone appeared, younger and prettier than the first woman. Shuffling along, he fell in behind her. He followed as she walked toward a bridge that passed over a nearby highway. Son of Sam waited until she was halfway across the bridge. Then he lunged forward. The first stab was to the head. The next three blows struck her body. Blood spurted from her wounds as she collapsed and fell to the pavement. Furiously the assailant struck twice more at her face. "Why aren't you dead?" he remembered thinking afterward.

While battling for her life, she screamed very loudly. Once more Son of Sam ran from the scene and headed off into the darkness. His victim, fifteen-year-old Michelle Forman, staggered off in search of help.

After the two Christmas Eve attacks, there was a seven-month respite. During that period, though, Son of Sam bought a gun, a .44-caliber Bulldog, a better weapon for the killing he felt he had to do. He soon put it to that very grim purpose.

On July 28, 1976, Son of Sam got a signal from the demons that he should strike again. "Blood!" the voices shouted in his head. He drove to the northern part of New York City, the borough of the Bronx. Slowly he cruised along the quiet streets, looking to satisfy his compulsion to spill blood. At about 1:00 A.M. he spied Donna Lauria, age nineteen, a medical technician, chatting in a car with her friend Jody Valenti, also nineteen, a student nurse.

Son of Sam drove around the corner and parked. He walked back to the girls' car, carrying the gun in a paper bag. When he was opposite the two women he whipped out the gun, crouched, and quickly fired five shots.

One bullet slammed into Donna's neck. She died within seconds. Another came to rest in Jody's thigh. She screamed and leaned heavily on the car's horn. With the girl's cries and the blaring horn ringing in his ears, Son of Sam raced back to his car. He drove off at high speed.

Although he was not sure he had killed both girls, he was pleased with himself. "You just felt very good after you did it," he later wrote. "It just happens to be satisfying, to get the source of the blood."

Nearly three months later Son of Sam heard the voices again. This time it was the "Blood Monster" who sent him out. As before, he weaved in and out of streets, looking for a victim. He sighted his quarry in Queens, in eastern New York City. Two people in a car had stopped for a traffic light in front of him. The killer was struck by the beauty of the driver's long, wavy hair.

Son of Sam followed them until they parked. He found a space for his car around the corner and walked back. Rosemary Keenan, age nineteen, a college student, was in the driver's seat. Carl Denaro, twenty, about to enter the U. S. Air Force, was seated next to her. They never saw the assassin take out the .44, pump five shells through the closed car window, and vanish.

Only one bullet found its mark. The slug struck the back of Carl's head. After two months in the hospital and the replacement of part of his skull by a metal plate, Carl was released and attempted to resume his life.

On the evening of November 26 two school girls— Donna DeMasi, age sixteen, and Joanne Lomino, age eighteen—were standing on the steps of Donna's house in Queens after a night at the movies. Just before midnight they noticed a "spooky" man watching them. The man walked toward them, reached into his jacket, and pulled out a gun. A burst of fire spat out the end of the barrel. A bullet shattered Joanne's spine. Another spark, and the base of Donna's neck was ripped open. Both girls toppled off the steps and into the bushes as the man fired three more shots at the house.

Donna recovered. Joanne remains permanently paralyzed.

"It was just like it should be," the killer said. "You shot them, and they fell. It was as simple as that."

Son of Sam went home, satisfied that the demons were at rest.

By midnight, January 29, 1977, Son of Sam was again prowling the streets of Queens, having parked his car. A couple—Christine Freud, age twenty-six, a secretary, and John Diel, age thirty, a bartender—hurried past him. Son of Sam noticed Christine's attractive long, dark hair. "Get her. Get her and kill her!" the voices in his head called.

He turned and followed the couple. They got into a car. Christine leaned over to kiss John. A clamorous din rose in Son of Sam's head as he watched from behind a tree. When Christine sat up, Son of Sam walked over to the car. Holding the gun with two hands, he aimed straight at her head. Three shots, and he was sure he had killed her. "The voices stopped. I satisfied the demons' lust," he thought.

On March 8, 1977, the fiends in his mind were raging once more. Again he drove toward Queens. "I picked Queens because there are a lot of pretty women there," he later told police. Leaving the car, he walked the streets until he saw college student Virginia Voskerickian, age twenty, approaching. When they were a few feet apart, Son of Sam stopped, aimed the gun, and fired point-blank at her face. She died instantly.

Just over five weeks later Son of Sam was cruising in the Bronx. At three o'clock on the morning of April 17 he saw a couple embracing. They were dark-haired Valentina Suriani, age eighteen, an acting student, and Alexander Evan, age twenty, a helper on a tow truck. With four shots Son of Sam took two more lives.

This time, though, he did not just disappear after the murder. He left a letter at the scene. It was addressed to

Police Captain Joseph Borelli. Borelli had recently stated that the killer had a strong hatred of women.

"I am deeply hurt," the note read, "by your calling me a woman hater. I am not. But I am a monster. I am the 'Son of Sam.'"

The letter appeared in the press. The name Son of Sam was on everyone's lips. Young New Yorkers, especially women, hesitated to venture out of their homes at night. Discos, theaters, and restaurants suffered big drops in business. Since Son of Sam's female victims had long, dark hair, many beauticians were kept busy cutting hair and changing brunettes into blondes.

Judy Placido, an eighteen-year-old student, knew about Son of Sam. As she sat in the car during the early hours of Sunday morning, June 26, talking with Sal Lupo, whom she had just met, she said, "The Son of Sam is really scary. The way that guy comes out of nowhere. You never know where he'll hit next. But what are you supposed to do? You just can't stay home forever."

At that moment Judy heard an echoing in the car and a banging in her ears. But she felt no pain. Sal felt something hit his right arm. He thought someone had thrown a rock through the car window. Later doctors found that Judy had been hit by three bullets—in the back of the neck, the shoulder, and the right temple. And one bullet was found lodged in Sal's right forearm. Both survived.

By now Son of Sam had presented his devils with a good number of blood offerings, but he simply could not stop their demands for more. At about 2:00 A.M. on July 31 he traveled to Brooklyn to carry out his latest order. Since there were no parking spots, he left the car at a fire hydrant.

While wandering around, he noticed a ticket on his car. Nevertheless he continued his quest until he spied his target couple, Stacy Moskowitz, age twenty, an office worker, and Robert Violante, also twenty, a clothing salesman.

The murderer watched from the shadows as they walked to their parked car. Many other cars were around; some had people in them. But Son of Sam could not refuse the howling devils. The crouch. Three shots. One to the head killed Stacy instantly. Two to the face left Robert blind forever.

The police officers from Operation Omega streaked to the scene. There were witnesses. Everyone was questioned. They scoured the area, but Son of Sam was nowhere to be found.

Some days later a witness recalled seeing a parked car getting a ticket just before the killing. The detectives traced the car. It belonged to someone named David Berkowitz.

An extensive check of the records showed that Berkowitz was born on June 1, 1953, as Richard Falco, but was put up for adoption soon afterward. Nat and Pearl Berkowitz adopted the infant and changed his name to David Berkowitz. The police picked him up on August 10, 1977, outside his home in Yonkers. By now they were quite sure that David was indeed Son of Sam.

As detectives and psychiatrists examined him, they realized that Berkowitz bore little resemblance to the make-believe character he thought himself to be. The man lived in a fantasy world in which he was clever, strong, handsome, successful, and extremely attractive. He told officials that Sam was the leader of the demons that lived in his mind. He said Sam had "been around since the beginning of recorded time." On earth, the "devil" Sam inhabited the body of Sam Carr, an elderly neighbor whom David knew very slightly. And since

David was under the control of Sam, he called himself Son of Sam.

A team of experts tested Berkowitz to determine whether he was sane enough to stand trial. They decided he was. In court he pleaded guilty to six murders and nine attempted murders. The judge condemned him to a total of 365 years in jail. Today Berkowitz is serving this sentence as prisoner number 78-A-1976 at the Attica Correctional Facility in Attica, New York.

Bibliography

These books tell about specific bizarre murders:

Bugliosi, Vincent, with Curt Gentry. *Helter Skelter* (Charles Manson). New York: Norton, 1974.

Cross, Roger. *The Yorkshire Ripper* (Peter Sutcliffe). New York: Dell, 1981.

Cullen, Tom. *The Mild Murderer* (Dr. Crippen). Boston: Houghton Mifflin, 1977.

Frank, Gerold. *The Boston Strangler* (Albert DeSalvo). New York: New American Library, 1966.

Klausner, Lawrence D. *Son of Sam* (David Berkowitz). New York: McGraw-Hill, 1981.

Knight, Stephen. *Jack the Ripper*. New York: David McKay, 1976.

Lincoln, Victoria. *A Private Disgrace* (Lizzie Borden). New York: Putnam, 1967.

Livsey, Clara. *The Manson Women* (Charles Manson). New York: Richard Marek, 1980.

Rumbelow, Donald. *The Complete Jack the Ripper*. New York: N. Y. Graphic Society, 1975.

These books include accounts of many crimes, including some bizarre murders:

Dickson, Grierson. *Murder by Numbers*. London: Hale, 1958.

Gaute, J. H. H., and Robin Odell. *The Murderers' Who's Who*. Montreal: Optimum, 1979.

Henderson, Bruce, and Sam Summerlin. *The Super Sleuths*. New York: Macmillan, 1976.

Jones, Ann. *Women Who Kill*. New York: Holt, 1980.

Nash, Jay Robert. *Bloodletters and Badmen*. New York: Evans, 1973.

————. *Murder, America*. New York: Simon & Schuster, 1980.

Pearson, Edmund. *Masterpieces of Murder*. Boston: Little, Brown, 1963.

Index

After House, The, 34–35
Alexandra, Princess, 21
Alligators, 9–10
Amurao, Corazon, 62–64
Anderson, Sir Robert, 23
Arsenic, murder with, 54, 55
Atkins, Susan (Sadie), 69, 70, 72
Attica Correctional Facility, 88

Ball, Joe, 9–10
BBC, 20
Berkowitz, David, 81–88
   childhood of, 87
   evidence against, 86–88
   mind of, 82, 85, 87–88
   parents of, 87
   trial of, 88
Bjorkland, Penny, 10
Blake, Helen, 58, 60
Blomberg, August, 31, 32, 34
Blood, 16, 27, 31, 32, 70–71, 83, 84
Bodies, 9, 11, 12–16, 18, 33, 42, 55, 73
   See also corpses
Body snatchers, 13
Borden, Lizzie, 24–29
   questioning of, 25
   trial of, 27–29
Borelli, Capt. Joseph, 86
Boston, Mass., murder in, 57–58, 60–61
Boston Strangler. *See* DeSalvo, Albert
Bram, Thomas, 30–35
   pardon of, 35
   trial of, 34
Brunner, Mary, 67
Burke, William, 12–16

Carr, Sam, 87–88
Chapman, Annie, 17, 22
Chicago, Ill., murder in, 62
Clark, Sophie, 60
Corpses, 10, 12, 13, 16, 24, 33, 39, 49
Crippen, Belle, 36, 38, 39
Crippen, Dr., 36–40
   alias of, 39
   arrest of, 39–40
   suspicions about, 37
   trial of, 40
Crook, Annie Elizabeth, 21

Death, natural, 12, 29, 56
   sentences, 16, 34, 40, 52, 72
Derelicts, arrest of, 14, 44
DeSalvo, Albert, 57–61
   arrest of, 61
   confession of, 60–61
   questioning of, 61
   trial of, 61
Dew, Chief Walter, 38, 39
Docherty, Mary, 15, 16
Doss, Nannie, 53–56
   confession of, 55
   husbands of, 54
   questioning of, 54
   trial of, 55
Drenth, Herman, 10–11
Druitt, Montague John, 20
Drugs, 62, 67

Eddowes, Catherine, 19
Edinburgh, Scotland, murder in, 12, 14
Electric chair, 52, 65
Evidence, 17, 27, 32, 34, 39, 42, 44, 46, 49, 64, 72, 75–76, 81

Falco, Richard. *See* Berkowitz, David
Fall River, Mass., murder in, 24, 26
"Family, the," 67, 72
See also Manson, Charles
FBI, 64
Fingerprints, 64
Folger, Abigail, 70
Franks, Bobby, 41–44, 47

Graves, 13
Green, Harry, 50, 51, 52
Gresham, Edwin, 42
Grogan, Steve (Clem), 71
Gull, Sir William, 23
Guns, murder with, 10, 30, 62, 81, 83–87

Hare, William, 12–16
Hatchets, murder with, 24–29
Helter-Skelter, 66, 68, 69, 71, 72
See also Manson, Charles
Herbert Fuller, murder on the, 30–35
Hippies, 66–67

Insurance money, murder for, 50–52, 55

Jack the Ripper, 17–23, 74
theory about, 20–23

Kasabian, Linda, 69, 72
Kelly, Mary Jane, 20–23
Kidnapping, 41–44, 47
Knox, Dr. Robert, 13–16
Kreisberg, Dan, 50
Krenwinkel, Patricia (Katie), 69–72

LaBianca, Leno, 71–72
LaBianca, Rosemary, 71
Laurentic, S.S., 39
Lauria, Donna, 83
LeNeve, Ethel, 37–40

Leopold, Nathan, 41, 43–49
evidence against, 44, 46, 49
questioning of, 43–44
trial of, 49
Loeb, Richard, 41, 44–49
confession of, 47
questioning of, 46–47
trial of, 49
Log's boarding house, 12–13
London, England, murders in, 17–23, 36–39
Los Angeles, Calif., murders in, 69, 71, 72

Macnaghten, Sir Melville, 20
Malloy, Michael, 50–52
Manhunt, 65, 81
Manson, Charles, 66–72
childhood of, 66
evidence against, 72
predictions of, 68
trial of, 72
Marino, Tony, 50, 51
Measuring Man. *See* DeSalvo, Albert
Medicines, patent, 37, 40
Monks, Lester, 30–33
Montague the Ripper, 20
See also Druitt, Montague John
Montrose, S.S., 39
Morgue, 13
Moskowitz, Stacy, 87
Mullen, Mary, 58
Murderers. *See* individual names
"Murder gang," 50–52
Murders, mass, 32, 58, 60–61, 64, 68–72, 73–78, 82–88
Murphy, Joe, 50
Mutilation, 10, 17, 19, 20, 23, 39
Mutiny, 31, 32, 34

Nash, Capt. Charles, 30, 32, 34
Newspapers, headlines in, 9, 64–65
New York City, murders in, 50–52, 81–88

Nichols, Mary Ann, 17, 22
Nurses, student, 62–65, 83

Omega, Operation, 81, 87

Pasqua, Frank, 50
"Perfect crime," 47, 50–52
Poisoning, murder by, 25, 26, 39, 50, 51, 54, 55, 56
Poison gas, murder by, 11, 52
Polanski, Roman, 70
Police, 9, 10, 15, 17, 19, 24, 42, 54, 58, 64, 74, 81
  artists, 61, 64
  investigations of, 25–26, 38–39, 43–44, 46, 60, 64–65, 76, 86–88
Prison, murderers in, 10, 34–35, 49, 52, 56, 61, 65–66, 72, 80, 88
Prostitutes, murder of, 14, 17–20, 22–23, 66, 74, 78, 80
Punishment, capital, 16, 40, 52, 65, 72

Rape, 32, 61
Reporters, newspaper, 42, 46
Rinehart, Mary Roberts, 34–35
Roosevelt, Theordore, 35

San Antonio, Tex., murders in, 9–10
Scotland Yard, 19, 20, 38
Sebring, Jay, 70
Shooting, murder by, 10, 70, 81–87
Sickert, Joseph, 21
Sing Sing Prison, 52
Slesers, Anna, 58
Smith, Dr. Leroy, 65
Son of Sam. See Berkowitz, David
Spahn Ranch, 67–68
Speck, Richard, 62–65
  alias of, 65
  evidence against, 64
  trial of, 65

Stabbing, murder by, 10, 17, 20, 61, 64, 70–72, 74, 82
Strangulation, murder by, 9–10, 58, 60–61, 63
Stride, Elizabeth, 18, 22, 23
Suffocation, murder by, 14, 47
Suicide, 10, 20, 65
Surgeon's Square, 13, 15
Suspects, murder, 43, 76, 81
Sutcliffe, Peter, 73–80
  alias of, 78
  arrest of, 78
  childhood of, 79
  evidence against, 75–76
  questioning of, 78
  trial of, 80

Tate, Sharon, 70, 71
Trials, murder, 16, 27–29, 34, 40, 49, 52, 55, 61, 65, 72, 80, 88
True Romance, 53, 55
Tulsa, Okla., murder in, 53

Valenti, Jody, 83
Van Houton, Leslie, 71
Verdicts, guilty, 16, 34, 40, 49, 52, 56, 61, 65, 72, 80, 88
  innocent, 28
Victoria, Queen, 21
Violante, Robert, 87

Walpole State Prison, 57
Watson, Charles (Tex), 69–72
Westerburg, Julius, 33–35
Whitman, Charles, 10
Widows, 10–11
Witnesses, murder, 9–10, 25, 33, 34, 65, 76, 87

Yorkshire Ripper. See Sutcliffe, Peter

About the Authors

GILDA AND MELVIN BERGER, longtime enthusiastic fans of murder and mystery, bring together in this volume more than a dozen fascinating accounts of the strangest and most unusual killings in their files. Working together and separately, the Bergers have an impressive eighty published books to their credit. Many have won special recognition by the Library of Congress, the New York Public Library, the Child Study Association, and the Children's Book Council. In addition, their books have been widely translated, and excerpts appear in a number of anthologies. The authors live and work in Great Neck, New York, devoting full time to writing books for young people.